First Edition

Copyright © 2020 Christina M. Kessler
www.christinamkessler.com

Published by Kate Butler Books
www.katebutlerbooks.com

ISBN: 978-1-952725-14-2

It is with great love,
intention, gratitude, and joy that
I dedicate this book to

Stella & Hudson
Loving you and being loved by you is truly one of life's greatest treasures.
This book is my 'promise kept' to you. I did it! We did it together!!
You make my heart smile!

David
Life is better with you by my side.
Thanks for being someone who continues to choose to lean into life.
Yesterday has been our teacher, today is our gift, and tomorrow is what we make it!
You get me, and I love that!

Mom & Dad
Your love, encouragement, and example continue to shine brightly in my life.
I learned I can do hard things by watching you do hard things.
Thanks for always being in my cheering section!

Hi, I'm **Grace**! And I'm **Graham**! Have you seen our friend **Gobble**? We aren't quite sure how yet, but we are going to make this the best Thanksgiving ever!

There you are! Everybody, please welcome Gobble! He is going to be our Thanksgiving mascot!

Hey! Whoa, hold up! I just got here! What's a mascot?

"A mascot symbolizes something important," Graham explained. "You're a turkey. That makes you a great Thanksgiving mascot!"

This seems like a lot of pressure!
What does the Thanksgiving mascot do?

It's no biggie, Gobble! All you have to do is share with the entire world why gratitude matters. We want to do our part to make the world a better place, and we nominate you as the mascot for the mission!

Say what? The world?? You are going to need to find a different turkey! That is way too big of an assignment for me! How do I explain gratitude to the world when I'm not sure that I understand it myself? Also, don't you need something big to make the world a better place?

Nope! You need a small thing that can make a big difference, and that's what gratitude does. Gratitude is as simple as being thankful and appreciating what you do have instead of focusing on what you don't have.

This seems like it could be hard. What if I can't think of anything? Do I have to do it?

Gobble, you don't have to, you get to! If you choose to do it even when it seems hard, you will not only make yourself proud, you will show others they can too!

My Mom always reminds us that we can do hard things. We don't need it to be easy, we just need it to be worth it! This is worth it, Gobble! Just "look for it!"

Look for it!!!

Look for what?

you
can do
hard things

What you can be thankful for, silly! We remind ourselves to "look for it" because when you look for it, you'll find it!

The more gratitude you put into the world, the more that comes back to you in unexpected ways. It's what I like to call the "Gratitude Boomerang Effect!"

When my eyes pop open in the morning, I say "Thank You!" And right before I close them at night, I say "Thank You!" Then I fill everything in between with more "Thank-Yous!"

But Graham, what if there are days that I don't feel like thinking about the things I am grateful for?

You're asking yourself the wrong question, Gobble. If you ask yourself the wrong question, you get the wrong answer. Try this. Do you want to be happy?

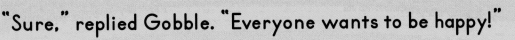

"Sure," replied Gobble. "Everyone wants to be happy!"

Well, get ready for your heart to smile because gratitude is like sunshine for your soul. Did you know that gratitude is scientifically proven to increase your happiness? Think of it like a science experiment for your brain and heart!

So, I can do this gratitude thing whether I'm happy or sad, anywhere and any time, by myself or with my friends?

Yes! Just remember, some days it will be easy and other days it may be harder, but you can totally do this, Gobble!

You know, Gobble, sometimes when I feel
sad and I decide to "look for it" anyway, it's
like turning on a flashlight in a dark room.
It doesn't change everything, but things
sure do start to look different in the light.

Gratitude

That's it! We'll call it The Gratitude Game! A game for young and old and everyone in between. We can make the world a better place one thank you at a time! We just need a jar, some note cards, a pen and, of course, some gratitude!

Note cards for everyone! Operation "LOOK FOR IT" is now in progress! Let's fill this jar up!

So, you really think I can do this mascot thing? How do you play The Gratitude Game and, better yet, how do you win?

You play the game by "looking for it," and you win every time you play. You'll see! What is something you are grateful for?

Alright, here it goes! I guess, I would rather attempt this mission and fail than to not try at all! I'm thankful it's fall. It is my favorite season. I'm also thankful for sweaters, hot chocolate with lots of marshmallows, and friends like you who encourage and believe in me.

Yes! Now, take it from your head and feel it in your heart.
Feeling gratitude changes you from the inside out!

Whoa!!! What happened to my feather?

I don't know, Gobble, but that is so cool! I wish that happened to me!

You want your tail feathers to change colors?!

Very funny, Grace! Gobble, what's something else you are grateful for?

LOOK FOR IT

I am thankful for my family, my crazy pups
Lucky & Champion, and my new ninja pajamas!

Wow, Gobble! I'm not sure what is happening to those feathers of yours, but it is pretty amazing! Let's see if we can get them all to change! What happened this morning that you are thankful for?

Well, I woke up, so that was pretty great! But then, I had to make my bed, load the dishwasher, and help my mom with some things around the house. That part wasn't so great.

Today's Chores

Make Bed

Load Dishwasher

Help Mom

LOOK FOR IT

Prepare to be amazed, Gobble! What would you say If I could help you transform the things you think aren't so great into gratitude?

"If you can turn my chores into gratitude," Gobble challenged, "I would definitely be impressed!"

Gobble, all you have to do is "flip it like a pancake!" Learn to look on the other side of what you think isn't so great. You get to make your bed because you have a bed. You have dishes to load because you have food to eat, and you get to help your Mom because you are a part of a family. See how things look different on the flip side?!

Wow!! I have been looking at those things through the wrong lens. I almost missed the good because I was focusing on the parts that I don't like.

You've got it, Gobble! Think of it this way, seeds have to be planted in some dirt before they are able to bloom into the flowers they are meant to become. Likewise, some of our biggest lessons are learned in the places we may like the least.

You two are the best! I think I might like living on the flip side! Everything is starting to look different to me. Nothing has really changed, but it feels like a lot has changed. I actually really want to think of all the things that I am grateful for!

Sounds to me like it's the perfect time to send up some gratitude fireworks! Let em' fly, Gobble! Tell us all the things you can think of that you are grateful for!

"Let's do this!" exclaimed Gobble. "I'm thankful that my Mom said she will have some freshly baked chocolate chip cookies for me when I get home . . . if my Dad doesn't get to them first!"

I'm thankful that I get to play sports and for my new tennis shoes that make me run super-fast! Lightning-fast!!

I'm thankful for family movie nights and for sure the popcorn that goes with it!

I'm thankful for laughter. You know the kind where you can't stop even when you try? That's the best!

I'm thankful for birthday celebrations, balloons, fun with my friends, and super cool birthday cakes!

I'm thankful that I'm creative and that I can draw, paint, and build. Give me a box, some tape, and some paints, and I'll give you back a masterpiece!

I'm thankful for summer fun! Bike rides, picnics at the park, swimming like a fish in the pool, and ice cream with all the toppings!

I'm thankful that I can sing and dance, although I'm not sure everyone else is. Hmmmmm . . . oh well!

I'm thankful for a healthy body and mind. I can do hard things, and I don't give up!

I'm thankful for trips to the mountains, hiking adventures, games, puzzles, and s'mores around the campfire!

I'm thankful for our family traditions, the memories we make, and let's not forget pumpkin pie with lots of whip cream!

I'm thankful for bear hugs, secret handshakes, and bedtime stories.

I know I said it before, but I want to say it again. I'm thankful for my family, even – I mean – especially my sister! Along with all the great people I have in my life who care. Like my grandparents, my aunts & uncles, cousins, teachers, and friends like you two are the best!

LOOK FOR IT

I'm really thankful you thought I would make a great Thanksgiving mascot. That reminds me to be thankful for boomerangs, flashlights, pancakes, and a new lens to look through, too!

Today is your gift, and it is waiting for you to unwrap it!

Don't forget to "LOOK FOR IT!"
When you do, you'll find it!
Let's do it together, okay?!

The End

One more thing . . .

Just for fun! A "Look for it!" challenge.
Did you notice that the "Look for it!" catchphrase was placed in many of the illustrations?
Next time you read the story, see how many you can find!
Some are super easy to find and others may take a second look. Enjoy!

See you next time! 💜
Love, Grace, Graham & Gobble

ABOUT THE AUTHOR

Christina Kessler is a born and raised Michigan girl who now calls Charlotte, North Carolina home. She considers it a blessing to experience life alongside her husband, David, and their two children. Christina is an author, business owner, and entrepreneur.

Growing up in a family and business environment built on success principles sparked an entrepreneurial spirit and love for personal development in Christina at a very young age.

You'll find Christina starting her day early, enjoying a cup of coffee, reading, writing, and carving out a little time for herself. She has learned that taking care of others well starts with taking care of herself well, first.

Christina is a cancer survivor. She says that getting to add the word survivor to that diagnosis has changed everything about how she sees and feels life. She lives out her reverence for life by creating a clear vision for the life she believes in and by making intentional choices. Christina says, "Today is a gift." As a daily reminder, she had that phrase engraved on a necklace she proudly wears around her neck.

Christina enjoys traveling. She loves a trip to the beach, but the mountains speak to her soul. Faith is the foundation that guides her life, and she believes that grace truly does make the world a better place.

Staying active is an essential part of life. Christina enjoys tennis, golf, hiking, and paddleboarding with her family. Fitness is also a mainstay, and she says nothing sets her mind in the right direction like a good workout! Running a marathon was something she proudly crossed off her bucket list. Christina's also completed the 4 day (48.6 mile) Dopey Run at Disney with her husband and sister-in-law. These days, her go-to sweat sesh is spinning on the Peloton (#CMK2340).

What are some of her favorite things? That's easy! Making memories with her family, chilling on the hammock with a good book, hydrangeas, date nights with her hubby, an afternoon spent painting, good food, inspirational quotes, shopping, meaningful conversations, and of course, mint chocolate chip ice cream!

To Connect with Christina or to learn more about her work, we welcome you to visit **www.christinamkessler.com.**

FROM OUR HOME TO YOURS...

Christina says she never set out to become an author, but she has learned to follow the promptings that are placed in her heart. Gobble and the book, "The Gratitude Game" came from wanting to instill a heart of gratitude into her young children during the Thanksgiving holiday season.

What started with Christina's children soon became something she knew she wanted to share with other parents, so their families could experience it, too!

It began with a simple turkey made from construction paper. Christina and her family simply wrote what they were grateful for on each of the feathers throughout the month of November. The construction paper turkey joined them at the Thanksgiving table, and they read what everyone wrote. It was a simple gesture, but it had worked!

The following year Christina got creative, and the turkey got an upgrade and a name! Christina doesn't even like to sew on a button, but she hand-stitched Gobble 2.0 to life! This version was complete with a gratitude jar and notecards and was placed on their kitchen island as a visible reminder to, "Look for it!". Gobble 2.0 joined them at the Thanksgiving table as they read all the gratitude-filled notecards written throughout the month. It was the perfect ending to a holiday that can sometimes be overlooked. Not only had gratitude come to life in their home, but they had also begun a family tradition that they love and look forward to each year!

Gobble is a friend that brings gratitude to life in a way that children want to connect with and can understand. Christina says, "Most importantly, gratitude changed from an explanation to something their family could put into action and experience in a much more tangible way."

To read more about Gobble, see some blast from the past photos, and find out more about adopting a Gobble for your family, visit **www.christinamkessler.com.**